ESCAPING THE MARRIAGE CONTRACT

MAIL ORDER BRIDES OF FORT RIGGINS

SUSANNAH CALLOWAY

PERSONAL WORD FROM THE AUTHOR

Dearest Readers,

Thank you so much for choosing one of my books. I am proud to be a part of the team of writers at Tica House Publishing who work joyfully to bring you stories of hope, faith, courage, and love. Your kind words and loving readership are deeply appreciated.

I would like to personally invite you to sign up for updates and to become part of our **Exclusive Reader Club**—it's completely Free to join! We'd love to welcome you!

Much love,

Susannah Calloway

VISIT HERE to Join our Reader's Club and to Receive Tica House Updates!

https://wesrom.subscribemenow.com/

CONTENTS

Personal Word From The Author   1

Chapter 1   4

Chapter 2   15

Chapter 3   25

Chapter 4   36

Chapter 5   47

Chapter 6   56

Chapter 7   68

Chapter 8   79

Chapter 9   90

Continue Reading…   107

Thanks For Reading!   110

More Mail Order Bride Romances for You!   111

About the Author   113

CHAPTER 1

Serena set the platter of hot, sliced roast beef on the table. The palpable tension emanating from her parents set her stomach to quivering. Her father's expression, as he never could hide his emotions, appeared a mix of anger, anxiety, and sorrow. Her mother wouldn't look her in the eye, her face downcast.

Serena slid her skirts under her and sat in her chair. The silence replacing the usual dinner table conversation unnerved her. *Has someone died? Surely Aunt Mae is in good health, for we visited her just last week.* Serena passed the bowl of mashed potatoes to her mother, Violet, hoping to see a lightening of her dour countenance.

"Is everything all right?" Serena finally asked. "You both seem – upset."

Violet flashed a glance at Michael, who grimaced. "Your father has something to tell you."

"All right." The quivering in Serena's stomach intensified. "It's not Aunt Mae, is it?"

"No," Michael answered, not meeting her gaze. "I'm not sure how to say this, Serena."

"Just say it," Violet snapped, her tone suddenly harsh, her brow furrowed in anger. "You got us into this wretched situation. It's your fault."

Serena gaped, pausing in the act of filling her plate with roast beef. She'd never heard her mother speak this way before. "What are you talking about?"

"I, er, made a bad business decision several years ago." Michael still wouldn't look at either of them, his elbows on the table as he clasped his hands together. "I went into debt. Deep debt."

"And?" Serena asked, tense, growing scared.

"The person I owed the debt to, in California, promised to cancel the debt if I, well, I –"

"Sent his only daughter and child to marry his son." Violet fairly trembled from bitter anger. "Your father agreed just today."

At first, Serena nearly laughed in relief. Surely this was a joke, a prank her parents were playing on her. An instant later, reality set in. Violet's anger was all too apparent, Michael's expression all too guilty.

"You can't mean it," Serena gasped. "I'm to pay your debt with my *life*?"

"It's not as bad as all that," Michael retorted, forking meat onto his plate. "You're twenty-one years old. It's high time you wed."

"But to a stranger? In *California*? A *stranger*?"

"Arranged marriages are often quite successful," Michael replied, his tone so pious Serena wanted to slap him.

"I don't want to marry this man," she stated firmly, deciding that would end the matter.

Her father finally met her gaze. "You've no choice. You board the train in three days."

"You can't mean this."

"If you don't marry Henry Dunstable, I'm ruined."

"That's not my fault."

"Perhaps not, but I've made my decision. I'm told Henry is a fine gentleman and will make you a worthy husband."

Serena stared, helpless, at Violet. Violet pushed her food around on her plate, not looking up. "This is not my fault."

Her father sent her the look he never failed to deliver when she misbehaved or acted foolishly. Refusing to back down, Serena gave back, stare for stare, nearly choking on her fear, her rage.

"You must marry anyway," he snapped, merciless. "Soon, I won't be able to feed you. It's better you leave my house."

"Michael Stapleton." Violet banged her small fist on the table, making cutlery jump. "That's *not* true. You're treating our daughter like a worthless servant. Apologize right now."

Hurt and grief joined the anger and fear within Serena's breast. Her father clamped his lips tightly shut, his attention on cutting his meat.

"There's no need, Mother," Serena said through clenched teeth. Tears burned her eyes. "It's quite clear Mr. Stapleton no longer wishes to have a family relationship with his daughter. So be it. That man is no longer my father."

"Now see here –" her father protested.

"No, *you* see." Serena stood, hiding her tears, her anguish, with a stony expression and tone. "You made your choice. I'll now make mine. How much am I worth? A thousand? Ten?"

He grimaced. "It doesn't matter. You're still marrying Henry."

"You do this," Violet snapped, "and I'll never forgive you. Not even with my last breath."

"You want me to be in debt for the rest of my life?" Michael shouted.

"Yes," Violet retorted. "If it means my daughter's happiness."

Her father looked away, his jaw muscles bulging. "You don't know what it's like."

"You could have worked to pay the debt," Violet continued, her face red with fury. "You didn't. Now I'll never see Serena again."

Serena gasped, the implications striking like a hammer. "Oh, no. Mother, I can't do this. I *can't*. I'll find a husband here, in Boston, a good man, there has to be another way."

"The arrangements have been made," her father said coldly. "There's nothing to be done. I gave my word."

Her fists clenched to halt her hands from shaking, Serena focused on breathing, organizing her thoughts into something coherent, some semblance of being in control of a situation that long since twisted far from control. "I'll never forgive you, either."

Turning, she walked from the dining room toward the stairs that led to the bedrooms above. Behind her, she heard her mother say, her voice ruthless, harsh, "I hope you're satisfied with the way you just sold your own daughter. Perhaps you should have sold your soul. *If* you have one."

In her room, Serena sat on the edge of her bed, numbness creeping in to replace the fear, the dread, the desperate desire to run away. To leave her home, her parents, and flee. Anywhere. Anyplace. As long as she could choose her destiny, make her own choices.

Where would I go? To whom can I turn? Serena thought of her friends, half-wishing one of them could take her in, hide her. Despairing, she realized how impossible that was. Her close friends had their own difficulties and tribulations happening in their lives. *And they would be the first place he'd look for me. And drag me to the train in chains.*

"Serena?" Violet tapped on her door. "May I come in?"

Serena drew in a shuddering breath. "It's open."

Not looking around as her mother entered and then closed the door softly behind her, Serena half-heartedly hoped her mother had created an escape route from this terrible dilemma. Violet joined her and slipped an arm over her shoulders.

"You don't know how much I wish this hadn't happened," Violet said softly. "I'm so sorry. I can't protect you from this."

Tears Serena could no longer hold back rolled down her cheeks. "I know. No one can help me."

Violet took her hand, squeezing hard. "Be brave, my daughter. Have hope that this young man will fall in love with you the moment he sees you. You're extraordinarily beautiful."

"Beauty fades in time," Serena choked.

"True. But you have so much kindness in you, and a deep and loving heart. You have much to offer a husband, Serena. This man will see that, and he'll be good to you."

"How can you know that?" Serena demanded, her voice hoarse. "You can't, Mother."

"I must have hope," Violet murmured. "Or seeing you leave will break my heart."

Violet pulled her closer until Serena's head rested on her shoulder. "Have courage," she whispered. "If he is not the man you need him to be, you come home. I'll wire you money. You get on a train, and you come home."

Serena swallowed a sob, her arm sliding around Violet's waist. "Thank you, Mama."

"Please write to me as often as possible," Violet pleaded. "I'll safeguard money just in case."

"And Father? What will happen if I return?"

Violet chuckled. "The terms of the debt will be satisfied. You married him—he wasn't the loving man you'd hoped for. If none of them like it, too bad. You won't be forced to go back to him."

The night before Serena departed for the far west, she slowly, and without enthusiasm, packed her belongings. She folded her dresses carefully to place in satchels atop her shoes. Hats went on top, yet she suspected they'd be crushed no matter how much care she took. Books, bits of jewelry, mementos of her happier life, a framed artist's rendering of Violet, and precious glass baubles went into others.

Violet entered quietly, pausing to listen down the stairs, then silently closed the door. She held a small bag in her hand and wore a cautious smile. "I have something for you."

Serena eyed the bag with little curiosity. "What?"

"My mother gave me this on my wedding day." Violet pulled from the bag a strand of priceless pearls. She held them up before Serena's awed eyes, her smile widening. "Take them."

Serena put her hands behind her back. "No, I can't. Those are yours. You must keep them."

Violet made a small, vexed sound, then settled the pearls around Serena's neck. "They're a family heirloom now. Take them, though I should present them to you on your wedding day. I can't. Then one day, give them to your daughter on the day of her marriage."

Tears, never very far from the surface these days, ran and dripped down Serena's cheeks. Unable to speak for her sobs, she hugged Violet hard, weeping against her shoulder. Violet's arms tightened as she, too, cried.

"Come back to me, my child," Violet wept. "Let me know how you are."

"I will, Mother. I promise."

Though the calendar said the month was April, the lowering clouds and the relentless drizzle, the chill breeze, told a different story. *This is my new outlook on life. Cold, dark and dreary.* The hansom cab took Serena, Violet, and Michael to the train station. The emotional chill inside the cab pervaded, nor did any of them try to lighten the mood. Serena hadn't spoke a word to her father since that horrible evening.

The cobbled street outside the railway station was choked with buggies, wagons and cabs, people coming and going in a packed rush. Porters bobbed and dodged, carrying luggage, inspecting tickets, and pointing out what train was where. Serena, her stomach in knots, stepped down from the cab while watching the teeming crowd with dread.

Michael hailed a porter. "Take these bags to this train," he ordered, showing the ticket to the young man.

With her possessions taken, Serena swallowed hard, trying to track him with her eyes, but she lost him in the mix. "Where's my train?"

Violet took the ticket from Michael, glanced at it, then handed it to Serena. "It's written there," she said, taking Serena into her arms. "Bless you, Serena, may the good Lord watch over you always."

"And you, Mother."

Deliberately, she avoided meeting her father's gaze, and withheld her blessing from him. From the corner of her eye, she observed his face tighten briefly before he turned his back to her. Violet kissed her cheek, gripped her hands tightly. Despite knowing she may never see him again, Serena could not forgive him this betrayal. *I have no father.*

Her handbag containing some money, the precious pearls, and a locket with Violet's face smiling from within it, Serena turned to join the crowd. Her heart hammering, her grief sticking in her throat like glue, she walked away. Once inside the busy throng, she looked back.

Her mother had vanished.

Swallowing hard, as alone in the world as she'd ever been, Serena pressed on through the bustling wave of people, and soon discovered she had lost her way. Looking around, she failed to see any numbers on the many railway tracks that took folks into and out of the great city of Boston.

"Excuse me," she cried, waving frantically at a passing porter. "Where do I find this train?"

He looked at her ticket, then pointed. "That way, Miss. Third platform down."

"Thank you."

Gaining in confidence, Serena made her way to the platform, steam puffing from the rumbling train's stack. A conductor escorted her to the first-class car where she had a small, private berth awaiting her. Her first-class ticket included meals in the dining car as well as a bed she could lie down in. Not many passengers were as fortunate as she.

Sitting beside the window, Serena stared out at the train next door. A chubby boy made faces at her through the glass, yet she couldn't smile at his antics. She was once that young, that happy, that carefree. Little more than chattel now, she had no more say in her happiness or her future than a horse did.

If he's a mean man, and heavy with his fists, I'll leave. I take a train home again. Mother said so.

CHAPTER 2

I despise this time of year.

Trudging home through the late dusk, Tim exhaustedly stumbled over rocks and ruts in the dusty street. Five children suffering from flu symptoms. A cowboy dragged by his runaway horse, his right leg shattered. *He may never walk again, much less ride.* A baby boy delivered to a woman in her forties who already had eight children.

This is why I became a doctor? To help people? I'm not helping, I'm aiding and abetting in their misery.

Lamps shining in the front windows welcomed him home. He and his widowed mother, Josephine, had purchased this sprawling, two story home in Fort Riggins, Montana Territory, the previous year. He'd found an advert for a doctor to replace the town's physician, who craved to retire, when he and Josephine lived in Cheyenne, Wyoming.

I can leave a place, but I can't run away from the memories.

Tim climbed the steps to the wide veranda and entered the house. The scents of a ham baking teased him the moment he went in, forcing his stomach to rumble. He hadn't eaten a morsel since before dawn when he was called out to birth the baby. "I'm home," he called.

Josephine, small and handsome with her dark hair innocent of gray, popped her head from the kitchen. "You're just in time. Wash your hands."

Though a doctor, not a cowboy, Tim wore a black Stetson hat, forwent a frock coat for a plain shirt and a leather vest, and heeled cowboy boots. He set his hat on the stand near the door, removed his boots, and padded into the kitchen in his socks.

"Smells great," he said, kissing Josephine's cheek.

"Busy day?"

"New baby, cowboy who just lost his profession. And the flu has come back."

He rolled up his sleeves to wash his hands at the sink's pump. "Stay away from people, Ma. They'll make you sick."

"Pooh," she snorted, turning the frying potatoes in the pan. "I'm perfectly healthy."

"Until you get sick," Tim commented dryly. "The flu is passed through the air. You breathe in the germs and get sick. Stay home."

"Nonsense. The ham is ready, take it out and start carving."

Tim sighed, aware that arguing with Josephine was akin to banging his head against the wall. Useless and painful. Using a thick towel, he took the ham from the oven, kneed the door closed, then set the hot pan on a wooden block. Quickly slicing the ham onto a plate, Tim then took it to the table.

"What else, oh queen of the kitchen?"

"Pour the tea, thank you."

Over the delicious meal or ham, spiced fried potatoes, squash, beans and bread with butter, Tim remarked, "Don't you wish you'd had ten of me?"

Josephine shuddered. "Good gracious, ten children. You were more than enough. Why?"

"Mrs. Alderson just have birth to her ninth. I imagine number ten will follow next year."

"She's only a few years younger than I am. Poor dear. Her next oldest is still in diapers."

"She didn't appear too happy about another child to feed," Tim continued, forking ham into his mouth. "Her old man is as useless as a broken wagon wheel. They live in squalor."

"I know." Josephine shook her head. "I've taken them food, as do many of us in town. The church gives the family money whenever possible. You didn't charge her, did you? For delivering her baby?"

Tim sent her an exasperated glance. "Is that what you think of me? That I'd demand coin from someone who doesn't have it? She offered me a chicken, but I declined."

Josephine beamed. "That's my boy. Though a chicken could lay eggs for us."

"We have enough chickens, Ma. And aren't you giving extra eggs to poorer folks like the Aldersons?"

"You're not supposed to know about that."

"I know more than you think."

Tim downed two helpings of everything before he felt full. "Thank you, Ma. That was delicious."

"You're most welcome."

She wiped her mouth delicately with her napkin, her bright, pale brown eyes filled with an anticipation Tim didn't like seeing within them. That look made him nervous, as it meant she plotted. And he never liked it when she plotted. It seldom boded well for him.

"You know," she began, her tone innocent. "There's an agency that matches men with wives. I heard about it today."

Tim groaned, lowering his face. "Ma, stop it. I won't marry again."

"Pooh. You're too young, far too handsome to stay single. They're called Mail Order Brides. You should write to them."

"So they come in a mail bag?" Tim snorted. "Maybe there's a catalog I can look at first?"

"Don't be snide. You know there are few marriageable women in this remote town, Timothy. You *must* marry again. I want grandchildren."

"Then *you* have them," Tim snapped, feeling trapped, angry, and more unhappy than he wanted to admit to himself. "Marie was a once in a lifetime love. That won't happen again."

"You don't know that," Josephine replied with a sniff. "I loved her, too. I also grieve for her, you know that. But she'd want you to be happy. You know that."

"I do." Tim clenched his jaw, staring at the table. "She said it whilst dying in my arms."

Josephine had the grace to stay silent for a time. At length, she murmured, "Give yourself a chance at happiness, son. You can. If you let yourself."

"Maybe I don't deserve happiness. I couldn't save her." Tim's stare turned inward, gazing at the memory of his beautiful Maria. The bullet that stole her life had ripped open too many blood vessels. He'd reached her, his swift hands trying to stem her bleeding.

But he'd arrived too late.

"I don't want to talk about it."

"I know." Josephine stood, picking up plates, cutlery. "You never do. You don't want to face a life without her, a life where you might find happiness in another woman. Experience love, have children, grow old with her hand in yours."

Bitterness twisted his mouth. "You didn't remarry when Pa died."

"No. I didn't." Josephine set her hands on her hips, glowering. "There's a difference. I had you. And while you were a joy to my heart, your father wasn't exactly the epitome of a husband and father. You know that."

Tim winced. "Okay, that was a cheap shot. Sorry."

"Too many men think with their fists." Josephine turned to the sink, and pumped water. "I didn't need another husband to beat me, hit my child. That's not a risk you'd face with a new wife."

"Probably not."

"Go on," Josephine snapped. "Get out of here. Leave me to clean up, and revel in my rotten memories."

Tim stood up, crossed the kitchen to wrap his arms around her. He kissed her cheek. "I love you. You're a great mother."

"And you're a disappointment. Go. Light a fire in the hearth, it'll be cold tonight."

"Yes, ma'am."

The house's previous owner had been a hunter before he died, and all his possessions remained within it after its sale. Thus, the skins of bears, elk, deer, antelope, wolves, foxes and no few rabbits covered the wooden floor and the rich furniture. Trophy heads were mounted to the walls, but Tim and Josephine had added their own touch to the vast front room.

Pillars made from tree trunks held up the expansive roof beams that crisscrossed the high ceiling. Four bedrooms lay on the second floor with a guest room just down the hall from the kitchen on the main level. A deep root cellar under the kitchen floor kept meat from spoiling even in the high summer. Behind the big house was a barn, a smokehouse, a vegetable garden, and a small corral where Tim's only horse dined on hay.

In the vast room where he sat, shelves held books, sideboards made of pale ash held artwork and fine trays of silver. A silk tapestry from Europe depicted a cougar chasing an antlered bull elk across a mountain's ridge. The wood-paneled walls added a warm glow as Tim lit a fresh fire in the hearth. Once it had taken hold, he filled a glass of fine Scotch whiskey from a decanter into a glass.

Sitting moodily by the blaze, he saw Maria's laughing dark eyes, her broad smile, tasting the bitterness of loss along with the molten gold on his tongue. *I miss you, my love. I miss you every day. What do I do? Tell me, please. What do I do? I'm afraid to love again, but Ma's right. I should move on, marry, have babies.*

Shutting his eyes against the sight of her bloody smile, her fingers raised to his cheek, he couldn't stop her whispering voice in his mind, his memory. *I'm so cold, Tim. So cold.* His own frantic reply, *You are gonna be all right, stay with me, stay with me, no, no, look at me, Maria. Look at me.*

Maria didn't stay with him. Her last murmured words were of his happiness, not her approaching death. *I'm – home. Be happy – Tim. Be safe.*

Then she slipped away while he held her in his arms, pleading, weeping, ordering her to stay with him, even as her lifeless eyes stared past him into nothing. Maria left him behind, gone to heaven, God, or wherever a human's soul went to after the body's death.

Sipping his whiskey, the fire's heat sinking into his bones, Tim pondered, as he did nearly every evening since Maria's death, his future without her. When she spoke on her dying breath that she wanted his happiness, did that mean happiness in another woman's arms? Or to come to grips with her death, and live happily alone and single?

"You weren't exactly specific, Maria," he muttered thickly. "Maybe I can't ever be happy without you."

You can.

Tim sat up straight at the ghostly whisper inside his head. "Maria?"

He received no answer. His skin tingled as though thousands of fireflies danced upon it, his scalp feeling as though phantom fingers roamed through his thick, russet hair. Tim knew he was no longer alone. But how could his long dead wife return to speak to him, to touch him?

"Not possible." His voice didn't sound like his own.

Sitting back, he watched as Josephine left the now dark kitchen, her small form ephemeral in the shadows cast by the fire, the lit lamps.

"Good night, Tim," she murmured. "Get some sleep."

Tim accepted her kiss to his brow with a smile. "Pleasant dreams."

"You as well."

Taking a lamp, Josephine climbed the wide staircase to the second floor, her shadow wavering on the wooden walls. Returning to his whiskey, feeling its relaxing effects loosen his muscles, his weary mind, Tim forced his attention to the following day. A visit to an old farmer dying of tuberculosis. Another to a young boy, accidentally shot by his older sibling. To pay a call on the cowboy who still rested, under the heavy dosage of laudanum, in his office.

"Evil never sleeps," Tim murmured, growing sleepy, his eyes closing. "Nor does pain, nor her sister, misfortune."

He woke much later; the fire had died down to coals. Rising stiffly, Tim added wood, blew the flames alive, then dowsed all the lamps but one. Taking it, his eyes and mind bleary, he climbed the stairs to his own room. Not bothering to undress, he crawled into his comfortable bed, shivering with cold, and promptly fell asleep.

And dreamed of Maria's smile.

CHAPTER 3

"May we join you?"

Serena glanced up at the elderly couple standing beside her table. She recognized them, as she did many other passengers who came to the dining car for meals since starting this journey. In keeping to herself, she seldom spoke more than a simple *hello,* or *excuse me,* and thus didn't know any of them. "Well, I suppose that will be all right."

Hesitant, wondering what they wanted from her, she pensively eyed them as they sat at the table across from her. "I'm Serena Stapleton."

"I'm Mathilda Gardner," the older woman said with a kind smile, extending her hand across the table. "My husband, James."

"A pleasure to meet you." Serena shook hands politely, offering them a shy smile. "I've seen you in here."

"As we noticed you," Mathilda replied. "You appeared so lonely, my dear, we just had to come to introduce ourselves."

"Where are you bound?" James asked as the waiter arrived to pour tea.

"California." Serena glanced aside. "I'm to be married."

"I'd say congratulations," Mathilda went on dryly, "except I suspect the notion of getting married is as appealing to you as getting all your teeth pulled at the same time."

Serena chuckled. "You're very astute, ma'am."

"Is this future husband ugly?" Mathilda inquired. "Heavy handed?"

"I know nothing about him at all." Serena replied, picking up her glass of tea to sip. "My father is indebted to his father, thus I'm the price of the debt."

"Of all the silliest –" Mathilda, her mouth tight, glance at James, whose brows rose. "Good gracious, child, can your father not work?"

"He works," Serena answered with a smile. "He's the chief accountant at a banking firm in Boston. Not wealthy, but certainly far above poverty."

"And he'd rather sell his daughter than make payments on this debt?" James grumbled. "How ridiculous."

Mathilda patted Serena's hand. "If this son doesn't treat you as you deserve, Serena, you go straight back to Boston. Goodness, a lady as beautiful as you should have no difficulty in finding a decent husband."

"You're very kind," Serena murmured. "And, yes, I'll go home if this doesn't work out."

The waiter brought their meals, a salmon filet in sauce with butter beans, dark bread, and a baked potato. As she dined on the fine food, Serena made light, bantering conversation with the Gardners. Her dour spirits rose, her loneliness and feeling of isolation lifted upon laughing for the first time since Michael's pronouncement of her impending marriage.

"If I had such lovely green eyes as you do…" Mathilda sighed. "And your perfectly oval face, I might not have been stuck with this fellow."

"Here now," James protested comically as Serena laughed. "I fell in love with your pretty brown eyes. Like shoe buttons."

"Buttons?" Mathilda glowered. "That's hardly a compliment."

"It's a sincere one." James winked at Serena.

"Gracious, after forty years of marriage, I finally get a compliment, and I'm compared to a shoe button." Mathilda rolled her eyes. "How I'm blessed."

James, chuckling, kissed her cheek. In them, Serena recognized the strong, steady love they held for one another. The first hot flames of falling head over heels had died long ago, leaving behind a powerful bond that would last until death parted them. A mild envy filled her as she nibbled the last of her bread, suspecting she'll never experience what they had now.

The love of a good man that lasted until death, and beyond.

As the waiter collected their dirty plates and utensils, then poured a strong black coffee into cups, Serena gazed out the window at the gathering dusk. "Where do you think we are?"

James also looked out at the darkening plains, tall grass blowing flat under the wind from the train's passage. "Illinois, I think. We'll eventually cross the Dakota Territory before dropping back southward toward Colorado."

"We're moving to Denver," Mathilda confided. "The East is so bad for his health. His doctor told him he needs a dryer climate for his lungs."

"Do you have family in Denver?" Serena asked, still staring out the window.

"Our son and his family." Mathilda sighed. "They're in the process of buying a house for us near theirs. Of course, we can't live with his wife." Mathilda's lips pouted in a small moue of distaste. "We never got on with her, you know. She's terribly mean-spirited, selfish, vindictive. She's raising the children to be the same way."

"How terrible."

"Our son doesn't see it that way," James added. "He's always gone, always at work. And he believes she's a good mother, so he doesn't protest."

"That's a pity," Serena commented. "I'd think kindness, generosity, and compassion are far more important than bitterness and hate."

Mathilda beamed. "If you'd married my son, I'd be the proudest mother-in-law. Come to Denver with us, do. James and I will find you a man who'll love you, and who'll be as kind as you are."

Serena blushed, both flattered and pleased at this statement. "That's so very nice of you, Mathilda. I can't accept such an offer."

"Why ever not?"

"I am obligated to wed this Henry fellow, for my father's sake."

Mathilda snorted. "You owe no one any obligation, child."

"I do. While I may no longer consider him my father, and am now estranged from him, I must do as he wishes."

"The girl has a point," James said on a sigh. "Besides, we don't know anyone in Denver."

Mathilda glared. "We'll *meet* people. And *those* people know people."

"Oh. Right." James smiled. "At least consider it, Serena. We'd love to have you stay with us."

"You're both so kind, and you barely know me."

"We know you well enough," Mathilda retorted with a sniff. "A frightened girl very far from her home. And traveling to the home of a stranger. I'd much rather see you wed to a man you've met, whom you know to be kind and loving, with a good chance that you'll love him and he you."

The Gardners repeated their offer of a home for her in Denver over the next few days as the three of them grew into close friends. Serena dined with them at every meal, regarded them as the grandparents she'd never known.

"No one would find me in Denver," Serena mused over a cup of hot tea with Mathilda. "Would I be wicked if I did live with you until I found a husband?"

"Of course not," Mathilda replied. "You're being forced into this marriage against your will. We're offering you a means to escape it."

"My mother would be so worried," Serena added. "I'd have to find a way to let her know how and where I am. She won't tell my father."

"We can get word to her."

Considering their most generous offer, Serena liked the idea more and more. *They're right; it's the escape I'd hoped for when Father told me I must marry this man.* Thoroughly enjoying the Gardners' company, envying them the long love they held for one another for nearly forty years, she laughed at their tales of their marriage.

Mathilda leaned over the table conspiratorially one afternoon. "Well, if James hadn't, well, you know –"

The dining car shuddered. The train's abrupt attempt to brake created a harsh squealing that grated on Serena's ears. Thrown forward, she struck the table's top, scattering cups and glasses everywhere. The Gardners fell back against their chairs as crockery and cutlery flew around the car in a wild crash.

Someone screamed. Men shouted, demanding to know what happened. Many voices were hardly heard over the sharp cry of the brakes.

"What's going on?" James demanded, holding Mathilda close around her shoulders.

"What's happening?" another man yelled as a porter ran through the car toward the front of the train.

The porter didn't pause, answer, or look back.

Serena slid open the window beside her, poking her head out to look forward. "There are men on horses," she said, fear jolting through her heart. "Their faces are covered."

"It's a robbery," James cried, his expression grim.

His words bounced through the car, repeated over and over as panic ensued. Women, and a few men, charged from the car to run toward their berths, many screaming about hiding cash, valuables, jewelry. Serena gasped in horror as she thought of her mother's pearls.

"Quick," James snapped, grabbing Mathilda's hand. "Take your ring off, earrings, too. Give them to me."

Mathilda obeyed, stripping her wedding ring with its diamond from her finger. Looking around for any robbers, James bent over to hide them in his sock, hidden by his trousers. Opening her handbag, Serena stuffed the pearls down her bodice, her fingers making sure there wasn't a bulge where there shouldn't be one.

An instant later, the far door slid violently open. A woman screamed. Serena stared, shocked, petrified with fear, as two men, six-guns in their hands and bandanas hiding their faces, entered the dining car. As in the dime books she'd read back home, they wore heavy long coats, dark hats pulled low over their eyes.

"All right," said one, strutting down the main aisle. "This is a robbery, as you might have guessed. Give us your cash, your valuables, and we'll leave you in peace. Put what you got into this bag."

He opened the neck of a cloth bag, then paced among the first-class car, offering it to the passengers. One by one, jewelry, wallets, bundles of cash, were dropped inside. He arrived at their table, his dark blue eyes calm, detached, yet humorous.

"Hiya, folks," he said amiably. "I'm sure you'd like to donate to a fine cause."

Serena opened her bag and pulled out the money her mother had given her. The robber eyed it skeptically. "That all?"

"Y-yes," she answered, her mouth dry.

The man eyed Mathilda, his gaze flicking here and there. "Where's your jewelry?"

Her chin lifted. "I left it all at home for safe keeping."

"Wise lady."

He ambled on, encouraging other passengers to donate to his great cause. Outside, Serena caught sight of more outlaws galloping by on horses, perhaps on their way to accosting the passengers in the other cars, stealing their few valuables. Beyond them, she saw tall mountains topped with snow, thick forests below. *Where are we? The wild west?*

Screams and shouts of protest rose from the sleeping car, no doubt from those who sought to hide from the gangsters. Serena shivered, terrified the man might suspect she, too, had hidden her valuable pearl necklace. And knew exactly where they were.

"Thank you, folks," the amiable gangster said, walking back. "I appreciate your lack of a fight over a few rings, I do truly hate violence."

Looking around as he approached their table once again, Serena gulped, knowing, *knowing*, by reading her face, he'd realize that she'd held back. His dark eyes met hers, then skipped past to James. James stared at him in defiance, perhaps daring him to a fight.

A fight the elderly James certainly could not win.

He passed James without a word. Turning his chair to watch him more easily, James swung his legs around. The mild *ting* of metal bouncing off the tiled floor resounded through the silence. The bandit turned.

In horror, Serena saw what he did. What James saw, his flesh turning a ghastly pale. A diamond earring sat in the aisle, twinkling merrily in the sunlight.

"What's this?"

The man bent to pick it up. After a brief examination, he lifted his gun toward James's head. "I don't much like it when folks hold out on me."

He swung the gun.

It struck James across his cheek, sending blood and his old body flying to the floor.

"James!"

Serena screamed. Not with fear, but with rage. Instantly, she attacked the bandit with her fists and fury, clawing at his eyes, dragging his mask from his face. He fended her off, trying to push her away while still holding onto his pistol and his bag.

"Now cut that out –" he began, but his words ended when Serena punched him in the throat.

His eyes bulging, he strangled, fighting to get air into his lungs. He sputtered, coughing, choking, wheezing. Taken off guard by what she'd done, Serena struck him square in his chest. He didn't react, but her hand hurt like crazy. Shaking out the pain, her lips pulled back in a grimace, she drew her fist back to strike another blow to his vulnerable throat.

Her arm was violently yanked around. She faced the second robber, whom she'd forgotten about. He, too, lifted his heavy gun, and struck her hard across her temple and forehead. Agony flared for only a second before everything went black.

CHAPTER 4

"Tim! Tim!"

Boots thumped across the wooden porch before Tim reacted to the sound of his name shouted. His office door burst inward. Luke Baldwin, the sheriff of Fort Riggins, rushed inside, his thick graying mustache bristling and his eyes wild.

"We got a problem," Luke bellowed. "Get your horse."

"What happened?" Tim demanded, striding toward him.

"Train is stopped a mile or so down," Luke replied, grabbing his arm and pulling him outside. "Robbery. People are hurt. Go on, boy, get your horse."

First, Tim seized the medical bag he carried to outlying farms and ranches. Everything he'd need for an emergency was contained inside. Following Luke, not bothering to grab his hat, he ran down the steps. Luke yanked loose the reins to his dappled gray, then swung into his saddle.

Running down the alley toward his house and barn, Tim turned as Luke trotted his gelding in Tim's wake.

"Tie that to your saddle." He threw his bag to the sheriff, then crawled through the rails of his small corral. His tough, half-mustang gruella mare eyed him with no little alarm as he charged into her domain. Inside her stall hung a bridle, but Tim had no time for a saddle.

"C'mere, Crowbait," he crooned, grabbing her by her mane before she could escape him. "There's a good girl."

He quickly bridled her, then, her mane in his grip, vaulted aboard her bare back. Luke leaned from his saddle to swing the paddock's gate wide. Leading the way at a gallop, Luke hit the main street with Tim hard beside him. They forced wagons, riders, and a few buggies from their path to avoid collisions, leaving outraged shouts rising behind.

Smoke puffed over the trees as Tim and Luke left the town's limits to gallop over the countryside. Even before they struck the wide, grassy clearing, Tim heard the distant chugging of the train's engine. On its tracks, the train stood idle as people stood on the grass outside, some arguing heatedly, a few others kneeling beside a body.

The body of a young woman.

Luke's gray bounced to an uneven halt as Tim's mare executed a tidy sliding stop, her haunches bunched under her. An elderly pair huddled beside the young lady, whom Tim thought was dead at first glance. The old man's cheek had been torn, and blood had trickled down to his shirt.

Dropping his reins, Tim slid instantly down from Crowbait. "Luke, I need my bag."

He knelt beside the young lady, his fingers searching for a sign of life. Blood coated her face, caked in her hair, the livid bruise around the deep cut across the left side of her head and brow informed him she lived even before he found her slow pulse.

"She dead?" Luke asked, leaning over his shoulder.

"Not yet."

"Can you help her?" begged the old woman.

"Do my best," Tim replied, terse, opening his bag. First, he needed to know if she'd awaken, or if her head injury had put her into a coma. Waving smelling salts under her nose, he hoped for the sharp reaction of the lady waking up.

She did. Snorting, crying out, she fluttered her eyes open for a moment. Gladdened by this, Tim inspected each of her eyes. Her pupils reacted to the sunlight. "Can you tell me your name?"

"Her name's Serena Stapleton," the woman cried. "She's from Boston, going to California. Will she be all right?"

"Yes, I think so."

Tim cleaned her wound of blood so he could examine the gash. *She'll need stitches to close that, hope she's not vain because it'll leave a scar.* But sutures could wait until he got her back to his office. He had to know if she had any other injuries in the fall from the train.

"Can you tell me where it hurts?" he asked.

"Head," she mumbled, half-lifting her right arm.

"Anywhere else, ma'am? Your back? Ribs?"

"That monster hit her with his gun," the woman snapped. "Just tossed her out like she was garbage."

Luke stepped forward to push her back, calm her. "Just settle down, ma'am, let the doc work."

Tim gently felt Miss Stapleton's arms, her legs, feeling only firm bones where there should be firm bones. "Luke, we'll need a stretcher, get her back to town."

"Wait a minute." The old gentleman paced into Tim's view. "She's got to get back on the train. We're taking her to Denver with us."

"We are," the woman informed him. "Help us get her to her berth."

Standing, Tim glanced at the train's crew walking down the track toward them. "This lady isn't getting back on that train. Not right now."

"No, wait just one minute, young man."

"We need to get this train going," the conductor, flanked by the engineers, stated, eyeing the lady on the ground. "Can we get her aboard now?"

"No," Tim replied, his tone flat. "She needs medical care. Do you have a doctor on board?"

The crew looked at one another. "Nope."

"Then she stays. When she's healthy, she can board another train to her destination. Now do you have a stretcher by chance?"

The engineer jerked his thumb over his shoulder. "There's one in the baggage car. Get it."

The conductor left to trot down the train's flank as the old woman cried, "She has to come with us! Make him put her on board."

The old man seized Tim's arm, his expression stricken. "She should go with us."

"You're welcome to wait with her in town," Tim said, agreeable, his hands and eyes inspecting the gentleman's wound. "I'm sure she can travel in a week or so."

"A week?" The woman gasped. "James, we can't wait that long."

"I can put a few stitches in that," Tim offered.

The old man touched his cheek gingerly. "No, thank you. I'll be fine."

"Let me clean it, at least."

As the man's wife argued with the crew that the train can't leave without Serena, Tim dabbed alcohol on the gentleman's cut, which wasn't very deep and had stopped bleeding.

"This is my fault," James murmured. "Had I given them Mathilda's jewels, Serena wouldn't be hurt right now."

"Oh?"

"The bandit hit me," James explained. "Serena attacked him in retaliation."

Tim's brow rose. "Did she indeed?"

He chuckled. "Quite the little spitfire, too. Would have had him except the other one got involved and hit her. She's supposed to go to California, but we want her with us in Denver."

"Sir, right now she's staying right here in Fort Riggins."

James stared at Miss Stapleton, who'd lapsed back into unconsciousness, grief filling his pale, haggard face. "Will you let us know?" he begged. "Let us know how she is?"

"Sure. Write your names and where you can be reached. I'll get word to you."

James clasped his hand. "Thank you."

Beyond, Mathilda lost her argument with the crew, and wept. The conductor trudged back to the group with a folded stretcher in his arms. James swept his crying wife under his arm and led her back along the track. Tim felt badly for them, but his only priority was Miss Stapleton.

"All right, gents, let's get her onto it."

Luke waved his arm over his head at the porters milling further down the tracks. "Get the lady's bags, will you?"

Tim and the engineer gently placed Miss Stapleton on the stretcher. Tim checked her pulse again, finding it strong and steady. She breathed easily, a good sign. He looked up at Luke. "Ride back to town. Get a few boys to help us carry her."

Luke saluted him, then strode to his grazing gelding. A moment later, he galloped up the hill and out of sight. The crew left him with Miss Stapleton, trudging through the long grass to the sound of the still-rumbling engine. Tim occupied his time with cleaning the young woman's face of blood.

Though pale, she owned exquisite, delicate features. Her eyes, when opened, were a lovely shade of green, quite beautiful in his opinion. Rich, dark brown hair had fallen from its previous coif and tumbled over her shoulders.

Serena Stapleton. Her name is as gorgeous as she is. Only the gash in her head marred her almost ephemeral beauty, but that would heal in time. Her bodice rose and fell with her every breath. Tim noticed her waist appeared so small he could place both hands around it and his fingers would meet. He smiled.

"A pleasure to meet you, Miss Stapleton."

The sound of legs swishing through the grass alerted him to the porters with her luggage. "Just put them down," he said. "We'll make sure they stay with her."

As one, the two porters tipped their caps, then turned to head back to the train. Only moments later, the engine's rumble deepened, grew louder. Tim idly watched as the train chugged forward, gaining speed, smoke puffing from its stack. Within a few minutes, it rounded and bend and was gone.

Stitching a wound while the patient lay unconscious made Tim's job much easier. The young woman's gash, while deep and jagged, wasn't long. He felt more concern regarding her brain and any damage to it than the flesh over her brow. He didn't like that she had stayed unconscious for so long.

"She sure is a pretty one."

Tim eyed Luke with annoyance, who watched the procedure over Tim's shoulder. "Why aren't you out catching those outlaws?"

"By myself?" Luke shook his head, his pale blue eyes avid. "I need a dozen men to chase after 'em, and that's a dozen I don't have. I'll wire the federal marshals in Billings, have 'em send a posse to run that gang down."

"Then make yourself useful," Tim snapped. "Go get my mother."

"Your mother? What for?"

"It's more appropriate to have a woman present when I have to undress this gal. Now do it."

"All right, don't have to get a burr in your britches."

Grumbling under his breath, Luke left Tim's office. Miss Stapleton lay on a narrow cot amid his desk, cabinets, bookshelves filled with books. It wasn't exactly a private place for a stranded young lady to recuperate from her head injury. Nor did he have to wonder what will happen once Josephine heard the story of the robbery.

She'd insist Miss Stapleton stay with them at the house.

"I suppose there's worse places for you to go," he murmured, cutting the last of the catgut. "I'm sure they took what money you had, so you can't stay in the hotel or boarding house."

Miss Stapleton made no reply. Rising, Tim washed his hands, then wet a clean cloth to finish cleaning Miss Stapleton's face. The last of the blood and dirt came away to reveal skin like fine porcelain over high cheekbones. Her lips were full, her chin dainty, and her closed eyes large. Tim couldn't recall ever seeing such a beautiful woman outside of his Maria.

The door burst violently open again as Josephine, followed by a resigned Luke, rushed inside his office. Her face contorted into an expression of worry and dismay, Josephine leaned over Miss Stapleton.

"Is she all right? Tim, she must come to the house, she absolutely cannot recuperate in here. Oh, the poor thing." Josephine plucked the young woman's hand from the cot and patted it. "What's the world coming to? What are you boys waiting for? Get her to the house."

"But –" Luke began, then visibly withered under Josephine's hard stare. "Where's that stretcher?"

Under Josephine's orders – *be gentle with her, Luke don't jostle her like that, gracious she's a lady not a horse, right, get her to the guest bedroom, it'll be easier for me to look after her* – Miss Stapleton was whisked to the house and installed in the guest room within minutes.

"Luke, step outside, please," Josephine snapped, her fingers at Miss Stapleton's bodice. "We'll get her into a comfortable bedgown."

As she unlaced the lady's bodice, Josephine lifted a pearl necklace from within the cloth's folds. "So those bandits didn't get everything of hers," she commented, then set them aside.

Tim helped Josephine garb Miss Stapleton in a light cotton gown, then covered her with a sheet and quilts. "She needs to rest."

"She's been unconscious for too long," Josephine said, tucking Miss Stapleton's arm under the quilt.

Just then, the woman's green eyes fluttered open. Tim leaned over her, studying her eyes, searching for any indication of deeper injuries. "Hello, Miss Stapleton, I'm Dr. Dawson. This is my mother, Josephine."

Miss Stapleton cringed, fear, no terror, filling her brilliant green eyes. "Who am I?"

CHAPTER 5

Snippets of conversations drifted through to Serena. *She's supposed to go to California. She's staying right here.* A vague sensation of being carried also slipped through the fog in her mind. Men's voices. Women's voices. The image of a young man with bright blue eyes looking into hers. *California* echoed through her memory, and with it the fear, the panic, of being sent there.

No! I'm going to Denver. I can't marry that man, I just can't.

"Don't jostle her, she's a lady, not a horse."

Serena woke to that voice, those words, yet didn't open her eyes. She realized she lay on a stretcher, and someone carried her. Her head ached with a terrible, fierce throbbing —relentless and sickening. *I must think, I can't think, they'll send me to California. What do I do?*

Drifting again into the painless void, Serena woke again as gentle hands covered her with a blanket.

"She's been unconscious too long," said the woman.

A wild idea flicked across Serena' mind, a way to avoid informing these people of where she was going and why. *If they don't know, they can't send me there.* Before she consciously willed it to happen, her eyes opened. The handsome, blue-eyed man smiled.

"Hello, Miss Stapleton, I'm Dr. Dawson. This is my mother, Josephine."

I should tell them the truth. But they'll send me to him! I can't, I just can't. Swallowing hard, trying to will away the fear, Serena choked, "Who am I?"

Dr, Dawson frowned slightly, leaning forward to look into her eyes. "You don't remember?"

Serena looked at Josephine, a small, petite woman wearing a gingham dress. She'd pulled her dark hair into a bun, and the same color of eyes as her son gazed at Serena with worry. "Where am I?"

"Our home, Miss," Josephine replied. "You were injured on the train."

"Train?"

Guilt at her deception rose to strangle Serena's throat. *It's wrong to deceive them, they're so kind. If they know, they'll send me to California to be married.* Dr. Dawson clicked his tongue, bringing her attention back to him. *He's so young to be a doctor, so good looking with those eyes and his hair. Will he send me away once I'm well?*

"Sometimes with head injuries," he said, holding her wrist to feel her pulse, "memories are lost temporarily. They come back in time, however." He smiled, and Serena forgot her pain for a moment, lost in the warmth of that sweet smile. "You'll stay here while you recuperate, Miss Stapleton. We'll look after you."

"I – I –"

"Now don't you fret," Josephine assured her, her hand on Serena's shoulder. "We found this in your clothes when we changed them."

She held up the pearl necklace Violet had given her. But the implications of what Josephine just said worried her far more than the pearls. "You – you undressed me?" She stared at Dr. Dawson in embarrassed horror.

He chuckled. "I'm a professional, ma'am. And I'm a doctor. My mother was here as a chaperone. Now how badly does your head hurt?"

Serena gulped, still upset that a strange man had taken her clothes off her. "Uh, it's all right."

He sighed. "The truth now?"

"Tim, don't badger her," Josephine scolded, showing Serena where she placed the pearls in a table drawer. "Give her a dose of laudanum for her pain and let her sleep."

The doctor scowled. "Just who is the doctor here?"

"Pooh. You know that's what you'll do anyway."

As though heavily put upon, Dr. Dawson opened a black bag on a nearby sideboard and drew out a brown bottle. He poured a small amount into a glass, added water from a pitcher, then sat on the edge of the bed. "It'll taste vile but drink it."

Serena obeyed, grimacing at the horrible flavor burning her tongue and throat. She gave him the empty glass, wishing she could rinse her mouth out. As though reading her mind, Dr. Dawson poured water into a fresh glass, and gave it to her with a wink.

She drained it. "Thank you."

"You need to rest, Miss Stapleton."

"Please, I'm Serena."

Horrified that she'd just exposed her false amnesia, Serena cringed, waiting for the condemnation. Dr. Dawson merely smiled.

"I'm Tim. No need to be formal, I suppose."

Serena smiled timidly back. "Thank you for helping me."

"It's what I do. Now get some rest. The laudanum will take effect rather soon."

Tim ushered Josephine, reluctant to leave Serena, out the door, but left the door partially opened. Lethargy stealthily crept over Serena's body, dulling her pain while stealing her will. Trying not to fight it, she nonetheless worried over her deception, her guilt and fear gnawing at her. *They can't send me to just any place. Can they?*

For the next two days, Serena did little save sleep, and wake to eat the food Josephine presented her, then sleep again. Neither Tim nor Josephine asked her many questions about herself, saving her the need to deceive them by lying. Still, what few dangerous inquiries they made were met with Serena's fear and a stilled tongue.

"You'll get your memories back," Tim said while examining the wound on her forehead. "You're healing well. You'll have a scar there, however. Does that bother you?"

"I don't really know," she replied honestly.

"With the way ladies style their hair," he continued cheerfully, "you'll have no trouble covering it. You know, just curl your hair over it."

"That's helpful, I suppose."

"How's your pain?" Tim lifted a warning finger. "The truth now."

"It still aches," Serena admitted. "Not as bad as it was, but if I move too suddenly, or sit up, then it throbs."

"That's expected. Your swelling has gone down, thankfully, and your bruises are turning an interesting shade of yellow." He grinned and patted her arm. "It means you're healing."

Serena couldn't help it. She smiled back. He had such a boyish grin and the sweetest smile she'd ever seen on a man. His blue eyes danced when he smiled, a trait that sent a strange shiver through her. No doubt, she found him very attractive.

Does he find me attractive as well?

Unable to discern anything from him save he was kind and a skilled physician. Even the way he patted her arm was the gesture of friendliness, not anything more. *How can I want anything more? I'm deceiving them both, they'll hate me if I told the truth. And I must get to Denver, and to the Gardners.*

As though he read her mind, Tim went on, "I wired to your friends in Denver. Mr. and Mrs. Gardner, right? To let them know you're recovering."

Stunned, Serena stared, caught off guard by his kindness and the fact that he knew of them.

"Oh," he said, "you were unconscious. And I'm sure you don't remember them. Yet. They insisted I let you back on the train to travel to Denver, but your injuries wouldn't allow it. But I promised to send word of you."

"Oh." Serena swallowed. She looked away. "They must care about me."

"Very much. I assured them of where you are, safe with my mother and me, and that you're healing."

"That's so kind of you, Tim. Thank you."

He shrugged with a grin. "Being kind is part of my job."

Serena wondered how she could get a letter to her mother, to let her know she was all right, despite being attacked by a western outlaw. Nor could she admit her deceit by asking to write a letter to the mother she professed not to remember. Upset by this terrible tangle of deception and the dreadful fear that drove it, Serena fought her tears, and lost.

"Hey, now," Tim murmured. "Things will be all right. I promise. You'll get on the train to Denver, or California, when you're ready."

"California?" Serena sobbed.

"Mrs. Gardner said you were from Boston headed for California," he explained quietly. "But they wanted you to go to Denver with them instead."

"Oh."

Tim pressed a handkerchief into her hand, then did something quite unexpected. He pulled her into his arms, resting her cheek against his shoulder. "It's all right, Serena," he whispered. "It's all right. No one will demand you leave here, you're safe, I promise."

Serena clutched him around his neck, sobbing, making her head pound terribly, but she couldn't make herself stop. Her tears wet his shirt despite the handkerchief pressed to her face. Distantly, the door creaked open, then Josephine's steps crossed the room.

"She's scared, Ma," Tim murmured. "She'll be all right."

"Serena, you poor dear. Don't you fret now. We'll take care of you, don't worry. It's hard being dependent upon strangers, but we're your friends. We'll take care of you."

Too weak and exhausted to cry for very long, Serena sagged back onto her pillow. Josephine pushed Tim aside to sit beside her, wiping her face with a cool cloth, murmuring soothing words of never abandoning her.

"You need sleep, Serena," Tim said, returning to the bedroom with a glass holding a dark liquid.

"Laudanum, again?" she asked, unable to protest.

"Just a drop in brandy," he answered. "I can't give you much more or you'll become addicted. Here, drink this down."

The brandy was almost as intolerable as the laudanum, but Serena drank it anyway. She craved the escape of sleep, fleeing the need to deceive these kind people, and to escape the nagging fear that should she offend them, they'd put her on a train to California.

And her waiting fiancé.

Feeling uncomfortably hot, she sought to throw the covers off. Shifting uneasily, her stomach churning in a strange nausea, she feared she might actually vomit up the brandy.

Josephine stroked her cheek with cool fingers. "Tim, she's awfully hot. Feverish."

Tim's firm hand cupped her cheek. "It's the brandy, I'm sure. Serena, you'll fall asleep soon. Try to relax."

"I don't feel very well."

"We just dumped a large amount of brandy into your almost empty stomach. That's expected." He chuckled, but Serena found little amusing in the way she now felt.

Curling up on her side, Serena closed her eyes, trying to ignore the nasty roiling in her stomach. Josephine tucked the quilt over her shoulders, then both of them left her room. Once they'd gone, she flung the covers off, hoping to find some semblance of coolness over her gown.

This is a punishment for lying. I shouldn't have lied. There will be plenty more to come.

CHAPTER 6

"She's terrified."

Tim eyed Josephine, then nodded his agreement. "But of what?"

"Isn't it obvious?" she demanded, picking up the paring knife to peel carrots. "She's a stranger, doesn't know how she got here, can't remember anything except her name. I'd be terrified, too."

Sitting at the kitchen table, Tim stared out the window at the quiet street outside. As dusk rapidly approached, townsfolk had gone home for the evening. Businesses closed. A few cowboys in town trotted their mounts to the saloon. Lights blossomed in windows as curtains closed. *I like her. I'm drawn to her, but I don't know why.*

"I guess that's a good reason to be scared," he admitted. "She's been traumatized."

"I'd sure like to traumatize that man who did this to her." Josephine jerked the knife over the carrot in her ire.

"Me, too."

"Will these outlaws ever get caught?"

"Luke planned to wire Billings and the federal marshals. He'll need help in catching them."

Silence fell between Tim and Josephine. Yet, an unspoken tension took the place of conversation. Tim knew what caused it and clenched his fingers around his glass of tea. *These outlaws may be the same ones who killed Maria.* But he could not say it. Nor did Josephine seem willing to mention that possibility.

Over her delicious dinner of beef stew, they spoke of safer topics.

"Will Serena get her memory back?" Josephine asked.

"In time. Blows to the head can easily distort brain function. Once her brain heals, she should get it back."

"Good. I'd like to know about her family. Or if she has family."

"What put her on that train?" Tim mused, biting into a chunk of beef with gravy. "What was in California that took her there?"

"I thought she was going to Denver."

"Well, her friends said she was bound for California from Boston," Tim explained. "After she was assaulted, they insisted she go with them to Denver."

"How odd." Josephine frowned. "Why change destinations mid-route?"

"Maybe they just wanted to look after her when she got hurt."

"That makes sense," Josephine admitted. "But I get the feeling that's not the entire answer."

Oddly, Tim inwardly agreed with her. Caring for an injured friend you just met on a train was one thing. Demanding that injured friend go to an entirely different city and territory was quite another. "Someone in California must be missing her. Worried about her."

"Until she tells us who that is, we can't do anything about it."

"No. I'm certainly not putting her on a train to the west coast without a destination," Tim declared. "Not if she doesn't know who or what is waiting for her."

Josephine glowered from across the table. "If you did, I'd paddle your bottom."

"I *am* an adult, Ma."

"So sure are you?"

A loud knock at the front door had Tim sighing in resignation. "An emergency, no doubt."

Rising, he left the kitchen to answer it, and found Luke, hat in hand pushing his way into the house. Baffled, Tim closed it behind him.

"Your ma's beef stew?" Luke inquired, his mustache at stiff attention. "Smells great."

"What brings you here? Is there someone who needs my services."

Luke hung his hat beside Tim's and crossed the sitting room toward the kitchen. "Not that I know of."

With another heavy sigh, Tim followed Luke's jingling spurs into the kitchen. "So what brings you here?"

"Luke," Josephine exclaimed. "What brings you here?"

"That's what I asked," Tim commented, resigned, and sat at the table again.

"Why, Jo, darling, that stew smells just wonderful," Luke said with a grin.

"Have a seat, I'll get you a plate."

As Josephine rose to fetch a plate of stew for Luke, Tim glowered. "So you came over to have dinner? Uninvited?"

Luke's eyes widened, his jaw dropped, in feigned astonishment. "Your ma said to come anytime."

"I did indeed," Josephine added from the stove, ladling hot stew onto a plate. "Tim, leave him be."

"I also came by to see how the young gal was doing." Luke looked at the loaded and steaming plate in front of him, then kissed Josephine's hand. "Jo, darling, I need to marry you."

"No, you don't," Tim snapped. "I sure don't want you as a stepdad. Anyone else, never you."

Josephine laughed. "I'm not marrying anyone. But you, Luke, you do tempt me."

Luke spooned hot stew into his mouth. "Cuz I'm so dashingly handsome."

"In what mirror do you look into every morning?" Tim protested.

Luke smirked.

"Serena is healing," Josephine said, sitting down at her place. "She still can't remember anything, poor child."

Luke scowled over his spoon. "So she can't identify the outlaw who hit her? Or any who robbed the train?"

"Why?" Tim asked, interested. "You have suspects?"

"The federal marshals do." Luke salted his stew, then shoveled more into his mouth. "They'll be here in a few days. They think this is the work of a gang called the Breyer Brothers."

"Tell us more," Josephine said, pouring tea from a pitcher into Luke's glass.

"Well, it seems this outlaw gang has been robbing trains all over Montana and Wyoming. Been at it for years. But they think the Brothers have a spy in the marshal's service who warns them the marshals know where they are. Right in time for them to ride for distant parts. So, the federal fellas can't catch 'em."

Tim looked away, his stomach churning. He dared not say what rose to his mind – *were these the same outlaws who murdered Maria?* Staring at his empty plate, he tightened his jaw, fighting the emotions that struggled for freedom, freedom to overwhelm him.

"Got something to say?"

Tim glanced at Luke. "No."

"Yeah, you do. But I won't badger you into speaking. A man's got a right to his private thoughts."

Josephine had the grace, and the sense, to say nothing. But, from the corner of his eye, Tim saw her watching him.

"So when might this lil gal get her memories back?" Luke asked, dipping a hunk of bread into his gravy.

"I can't answer that," Tim retorted. "Healing isn't a cut and dried process, you know that."

Luke shrugged, his jaws chewing his food rapidly. "Just thought to ask, no need to get a burr in your britches."

"Then next time you say that," Tim snapped. "I'm gonna put a bullet between your eyes."

"Timothy Dawson."

Hunching his shoulders over his plate, Luke smirked, then asked, "If that lil gal in there sees a picture, might that jar her memories loose?"

Nodding thoughtfully, Tim said, "It's possible. Are the marshals bringing pictures of the gang?"

"Wanted posters." Luke wiped gravy from his plate with a hunk of bread, then munched it. "They say they need a positive identification. And if this gal saw the Breyer Brothers themselves on that train, why she might be in for the reward money. Once they're caught, and if they're caught."

"There's a reward on this gang?" Josephine inquired, her eyes wide.

"Yup." Luke sighed happily, leaning back in his chair to pull his pipe and tobacco pouch from his pocket. "Mind if I smoke?"

Tim objected but wouldn't say so. Josephine quite liked the scent of pipe smoke, had often told him how it reminded her of her father. Tim never liked it, and strongly suspected smoking wasn't a healthy occupation.

"I don't mind," she answered, rising to begin clearing away the dishes. Filling a kettle, she placed it on the hot stove, then spooned stew onto a plate. Without a word, she took it and utensils out of the kitchen and down the hall.

"Why was Serena going to California?" Tim mused, absently watching Luke light his pipe.

"That's her business, I reckon," Luke said, puffing. "See family? Join family? Get married?"

"A Mail Order Bride?" Tim frowned as he considered this.

"A mail what you call it?"

"Ma told me about an agency that matches women from the east to men in the west. They find one another, get married."

"Now that's a strange way to get hitched." Luke shook his head. "You planning on trying it?"

"Don't be stupid."

"Your ma wants you hitched something awful."

"I was once. I'm not going there again."

Luke shrugged, pulling his pipe from his lips to examine in closely. "Suit yourself."

"I plan to."

Inserting the pipe between his lips, Luke mused, "You have a real pretty gal right down the hall in your guest room. Appears she's single, too."

Tim eyed him disgust. "Don't you have something better to do than annoy me?"

"Nope." Luke gazed back at him blandly.

Snorting, Tim glanced aside. He didn't like that he did indeed feel an attraction to Serena. That in holding her close, letting her weep on his shoulder, something within him had softened. Had loosened. As though an unknown *something* had nudged him into a specific direction. *I can't. I'll never love anyone the way I loved Maria.*

So?

Startled, Tim shot a swift look at Luke, half-thinking he had spoken. Luke fussed with his pipe, however, and paid him little attention. *Can I love someone else? Ma seems to think so. If I did, am I betraying Maria's memory? The love we had for one another?*

"Nope."

Tim tightened his jaw to prevent a gape of shock. *He couldn't have read my mind. He couldn't have.* "Excuse me?"

"Finding a wife through the mail," Luke went on. "Nope. Not right, no sir. A man and woman should have a chance to know each other, make sure they suit one another first." He chuckled. "Your ma sure suits me just fine."

"Court my mother and I'll remove your appendix," Tim replied darkly. "Very … slowly."

"My what?"

"Without laudanum."

Luke pointed his pipe stem at Tim, frowning. "Son, you have a right cantankerous attitude. How are you going to find a wife whilst being so doggone surly?"

"That's how I keep potential wives at bay," Tim replied. "By being surly."

Puffing his pipe, Luke shook his head. "We got to start changing that right now."

Tim gathered a sharp retort, but Josephine's return instantly stifled it.

"Serena is much better," she crowed, taking the empty plate she carried to the sink. "She thinks she'll be able to get out of bed tomorrow."

"I believe my opinion carries more weight," Tim commented dryly.

"Pooh. She should know how strong she is better than you, dear."

"I hate it when my patients think they know more than I do," Tim muttered, cross.

Luke smirked. Josephine half-turned, her brows hiked. "What did you say?"

"Nothing."

"That's what I thought."

Deciding the night's chill required a fire to keep it at bay, Tim rose to leave the kitchen. In the nearly dark front room, he gathered kindling into a pile in the hearth, then lit it. The new flames gobbled the treat quickly, growing in size and strength. After adding solid chunks of wood, he sat in a comfortable armchair to watch the fire flicker red and orange.

I miss her. The tearing pain of loss struck him anew, an agony he'd forced into his heart's background since Maria died. Can he go on without her? If so, how was he to accomplish the impossible? Tim swallowed his grief, his heartbreak, his pain, absently wondering what would have happened in their lives had she lived.

Was it time to let her go? Tim sniffed back unbidden tears, unwilling to consider that possibility. *How can I? How can I not? Do I go on like this for the rest of my life? Forever in mourning, never happy?* He considered that dismal prospect. A long life ahead of him filled with grief and memories and pain.

Is that what I want?

He half-listened to the banter emerging from the kitchen, then sighed. Standing, he added wood to the flames, then climbed the stairs to his bedroom. Undressing in the dark, he climbed into his bed.

And lay awake for a long time.

CHAPTER 7

The sun hovered over the eastern horizon as Serena opened a satchel to pull a fresh gown from it. The one she'd worn on the day the outlaws attacked the train lay over a chair, in dire need of a wash. It would take a lot of scrubbing to get the grass and blood stains from it. After donning a pale green gown that matched her eyes, her hair flowing loosely around her shoulders, she left her room.

The big house lay shadowed and silent as she ambled around the main floor, looking and admiring the furnishings, the vast space. Standing near a big picture window, she observed early risers striding down the street outside. A buggy rolled past, drawn by a stout gray horse. From what she could see of the town without going outside, it appeared a pleasant enough place, though not as exciting as Boston.

Hearing footsteps on the stairs, Serena turned.

Tim, dressed in a plain white shirt and blue jeans, his boots thumping on the wood staircase, smiled upon catching sight of her. "Look who's up."

Smiling back, Serena ran her hands nervously over her gown. "I feel much better, thank you."

"Any pain?"

He crossed the sitting room toward her. Serena's face warmed under his regard, no doubt flushing crimson, and replied, "I'm fine."

"Truth now." Tim halted in front of her, his fingers lightly brushing her hair away from her brow. "You're healing well."

"It's because I have a great doctor."

"Hungry?" he asked, taking her arm. "I'm not a great cook, but I can rustle up some breakfast."

"Why don't you let me cook for you?" she suggested, permitting him to steer her toward the kitchen. "I'd like to repay my debt."

"What debt?" He eyed her sidelong.

"For your care of me. The food you've given."

Tim snorted. "That's hardly a debt. But only because I'm not a good cook, I'll let you. Ma should be down soon."

Instantly at home in the kitchen, Serena inspected the contents of the cupboards and the pantry while Tim rekindled the fire in the stove. He then opened a trap door amid the wood planks of the floor to reveal a root cellar.

"I'll get some ham and eggs," he commented, then vanished down into the dark.

After cutting potatoes into a frying pan, the ham already sizzling on the stove, Serena glanced around to find Josephine entering the kitchen. Tim had murmured a comment about buying the newspaper and left the house a short while ago.

"Good morning."

"It certainly seems that way." Josephine, smiling broadly, inspected Serena's handiwork at the stove. "Smells great. I expect your cooking skills have returned to you."

Serena turned her face away, her gut clenching at her deliberate deception of these kind people. She said nothing, however, but wondered how she could extract herself from this terrible situation. *I must write to Mother. Beg her to wire money so I can buy a train ticket to Denver. I don't want to hurt Tim and Josephine, but if they find out I'm lying –*

Josephine turned the ham with a fork. "I'm going to hate seeing you leave."

"Why?" Serena asked, confused. "Am I not a burden on you both?"

"A burden?" Josephine snorted. "Hardly. I'm enjoying having you here, enjoy looking after you."

"Oh."

Discomfited, Serena had no idea what to say. She added salt and pepper to the potatoes, her thoughts scrambled, disconnected. *Is it possible for me to stay here, perhaps find employment? In time, find a husband of my own choosing?* On the heels of that inner question, Serena thought of Tim. An extraordinarily good-looking man without a wife, but with a steady means of income.

"May I ask why Tim isn't married?" she asked, tentative, worried she asked a question that wasn't any of her business.

"He was," Josephine replied. "She was killed."

Shock jolted through Serena. "Oh, I'm so sorry."

"It was terrible," Josephine went on, her voice low, facing Serena. "She'd gone to Denver to visit family."

"What happened?" Serena swallowed hard, unsure if she should hear the details.

"Outlaws stopped the train to rob it," Josephine said, her voice thick with tears. "Just outside of town, just like what happened to you."

"Oh, dearest God."

"Maria was shot." Josephine turned away, tears rolling down her cheeks. "Tim tried to stop the bleeding but couldn't. She died in his arms."

"That's –" Serena swallowed and started again. "That's terrible."

"Now we have to wonder if the men who attacked your train also killed Maria." Josephine wiped her face with her apron and sniffed hard. "Luke, our sheriff, says the same gang robs trains throughout Wyoming and Montana. We lived in Wyoming at the time."

"It certainly sounds plausible," Serena murmured, grieving for them, for a woman she'd never met. "They nearly killed me. They're vicious men."

"The sheriff has wired to the federal marshals," Josephine continued. "He wants to know if you might recognize the gang by looking at their pictures."

Serena uneasily recalled the face, the eyes, of the amiable outlaw, but only caught a glimpse of the other before he hit her. Still, she remembered his cold eyes. "I'll certainly try."

"If they know for certain the Breyer Gang are the criminals," Josephine said, "it may help them to find, and catch them."

"I'll do whatever I can to help." Inwardly, Serena had to ask herself – *if I do recognize him, does that mean I must drop the deception? Tell them the truth that I'm to marry a man in*

California and I'm terrified they'll send me there? That I cannot, and will not, marry this Henry person.

What will they do?

Later that day, as Serena cheerfully helped Josephine clean the house, wash clothes, feed the chickens and the oddly colored horse in the corral, Tim arrived home unexpectedly. With three strange men. A bolt of fear shot through Serena's heart as she met Tim's grim expression, saw the tension in him. Josephine slipped her arm through hers, standing beside her while facing the strangers.

"Serena," Tim began. "This is Luke Baldwin, our town sheriff."

A grizzled man with a bristling gray mustache offered her a kind smile as he shook her hand. "Nice to meet you at last, ma'am, though I looked in on you while you were unconscious."

"A pleasure, I'm sure."

"These men," Tim's hand beckoned the other two forward, "are federal agents. They'd like to talk with you, if that's all right."

Serena eyed the seemingly cold, stern men in dark suits and bowler hats they didn't remove while indoors.

"Marshal Keith Anderson," said the shorter of the two, shaking her hand. "My partner, Marshal Pete Harris. The doc here says you lost your memory. That right?"

Serena, shaking with fear, only stared. Helpless, she flicked her gaze among the four men looking at her, unable to say a word.

"It's true," Josephine snapped, fierce. "You marshals are frightening her. Now take off your hats and behave like gentlemen."

Abashed, the pair swept their bowlers from their heads. Oddly, they seemed less intimidating now, and Josephine's sharp defense gave Serena courage. As did Tim's encouraging smile and the sheriff's quick nod.

"You have pictures?" she asked, forcing calm into her voice.

"Yes, ma'am." Marshal Anderson pulled folded papers from his breast pocket. "If you don't mind, have a look at these. See if you recognize anybody."

Taking them, Serena unfolded the papers, fighting to prevent them from rattling under her trembling hands. At the top in large bold lettering was the phrase WANTED. DEAD OR ALIVE. Her eyes dropped to the sketch of a man's face.

And gasped in disbelief. "It's him. That's *him*."

Anderson almost pounced on her, taking the paper. "You sure? That's the outlaw from the train?"

"Yes. He seemed almost friendly, walking about, asking for donations." Serena looked lower and read the name – Gregory Breyer.

"How about that one?"

He took Breyer's poster from her, revealing a second WANTED. DEAD OR ALIVE paper. Serena frowned. She studied the cold eyes, unsure if that was the man who spun her around before striking her with his pistol. Lifting her hand, she covered the lower half of the face.

"Yes," she declared. "He's the one who hit me. I know his eyes."

"Harold Breyer," Anderson said, taking the poster back. "Both are leaders of the gang. Thank you, ma'am, you've been a great help."

Josephine hugged her close, smiling, and Sheriff Baldwin patted her on her shoulder. Tim, after seeing the marshals out the front door, returned to grin, and said, "Perhaps seeing those pictures will encourage the rest of your memories to come back."

Serena only nodded, thinking back to those terrible moments on the train, Mathilda and James, the Breyer Brothers, of fighting with Gregory Breyer after he struck James. "How will the marshals catch them?"

"Yours is the first positive identification, ma'am," Sheriff Baldwin said. "They kept their faces covered at all the other robberies, see. But you dragged his mask down."

"I did?" Serena frowned, recalling the fight, Gregory's protest before her small fist slammed into his throat. How did she see his face? Somehow, she saw it clearly even in her rage, her need to hurt him as he'd hurt James.

"From what Mr. Gardner told me," Tim said, grinning, "you're a little spitfire. Almost had that bandit on the ground if the other one hadn't knocked you out cold."

Serena blushed, looking aside. "No, that can't be right. I'm no spitfire. He's surely exaggerating."

"I don't think he was."

"Are you home for the day?" Josephine asked Tim. "If so, we'll start supper."

Sheriff Baldwin grinned. "What's for dinner?"

"You're not invited." Tim scowled.

"Yes, he is. Luke, Tim, chop some firewood and feed the stock, oh, and muck the horse's stall. Serena will help me in the kitchen."

The sheriff's face fell. "You mean I have to *work*?"

"Yes, now get to it." Josephine waved her hands imperiously. "If you don't, Luke, you'll get no apple pie."

"I'm going, I'm going, don't get a burr in your britches."

Both Tim and Sheriff Baldwin headed for the front door. "I really hate that expression," Tim complained as they went.

"Too bad, son, you have to listen to it. Especially if I marry your ma."

"Court her and I'll kill you."

The late evening air felt almost cold after the warmth of the house, especially the kitchen, when Serena let herself out to sit on the veranda. She'd enjoyed the camaraderie among the four of them at supper, laughing, chatting gaily. She almost felt part of the family as Luke seemed to be. Almost. Only her dark secret hung over the table like an unwanted spirit.

Piano music drifted from the saloon a few blocks down. Faint light gleamed from behind curtains in the houses around the Dawson home while Serena absently wondered who those people were, what they were like, whom they loved.

"Mind if I join you?"

Tim stepped from the light of the doorway, then closed it behind him, leaving them both in shadow.

"No, I don't mind."

Tim sat in the chair beside her. "A little chilly, eh?"

"It feels good, though."

"In a few weeks, the weather will warm up," he said. "In this high country, winter leaves late and comes back early."

Serena pondered Boston at this time of year, suspecting that even now the heat of summer had already moved in. She gazed up at the stars overhead, marveling at their crystal beauty. "The stars are amazing, aren't they?"

"I do agree with you there."

His hand slid over hers as it rested on the chair's arm. Startled, Serena glanced at him, but didn't take her hand away. Instead, she curled her fingers around it, squeezing, liking the contact, liking *him*. Liking how he looked at her over the supper table, how his eyes tended to rest on hers, his smile seemed for her alone.

Thus, when he bent his face toward her, Serena didn't flinch. When his mouth settled on hers in a tender, sweet kiss, she caressed the side of his face. And wondered if this was what falling in love was.

CHAPTER 8

Serena's returning kiss was innocent, inexperienced, even naïve. Tim liked how she curled her hand in his, holding onto him. He liked how she never recoiled when he bent to kiss her without permission. Most of all, he liked how Serena made him feel deep inside.

Warm, hopeful, filled with the wonder of exploring the possibility of love with another human being.

"That's nice," he murmured, admiring her face so close to his.

Serena chuckled. "My first kiss ever."

Instantly, she turned her face away as though embarrassed. Tim, his finger on her chin, swung her back to face him. "There's nothing wrong with that. You shouldn't feel shame for admitting you've never been kissed before."

"Thank you for saying that."

"Serena," Tim went on, inwardly feeling his way through what he should say and what he shouldn't. "I really like you."

"I like you, too."

Tim hesitated. "I was married once."

"I know. Josephine told me. Tim, I'm so sorry for your loss."

"Thank you. That you already know makes it easier to explain myself, I guess." He swallowed. "I find it hard to move past her, Serena. I suppose I must, if I'm ever to find happiness again."

Her fingers tightened. "You should do what's best for you."

"True enough. However, I like you. I know you're going to leave, take a train to California, or Denver. I still don't know which one."

He watched her perfect profile as she gazed up at the stars, perhaps thinking, perhaps seeking her wayward memories. "If I find what I seek here, in Montana, perhaps I don't have to go to either place."

"And what are you seeking, Serena?"

"Love. Hope. A future."

"I don't want you to leave," Tim went on, warmth and happiness rising from deep within. "Not until you regain your memories, until you know what it is you want."

"I don't want to be a burden."

"You're far from that, Serena. My ma adores you. Your being here has brought her so much happiness."

"Why?"

Tim sighed heavily. "Please, don't be offended by my answer. All right?"

"I promise."

"She hopes you and I might find love, get married. She wants to see me happy, craves to see me married again. Here you come, lovely and kind and she sees her future grandchildren dancing in your eyes."

Serena laughed. "That's not a bad desire, is it?"

"No. Not really. Except that until I met you, I didn't want any of that."

"And now?"

"I see possibilities. Sorry if that's not very clear."

"No, it's what I'm seeing, too. Possibilities. For what I hope for." Her free hand covered their joined link. "I see you're a very kind, wonderful man, Tim. Any woman would be blessed to have you as a husband. I'm simply not sure I'm qualified for the role as your wife, should we go that far."

"Why not? Don't you want children?"

"I want children." Serena turned her face away. "Once you know all about me, your feelings will change."

"Unless you murdered someone in cold blood, I can't see anything about you changing how I feel." He chuckled. "You didn't murder anyone? Right?"

"Of course not. But there may be a side of me you won't like."

"Will you tell me?" he asked quietly. "Someday?"

"Someday. Yes."

"Then I'll wait for you to tell me. Meanwhile, let's get to know one another. Will that be all right?"

"I'd like that, Tim. Very much."

His spirits high for the first time since Maria died, Tim delved into his work the following day, dispensing medicine and advice in equal measure to the folks of Fort Riggins. He set a young boy's broken arm after the kid fell from a tree, doled out medicine for the flu, inspected old man Chalmers's bout of gout.

The day nearly over, Tim straightened his office for the following day, made notes on what he needed to order, and turned in surprise when Luke entered his office.

"You catch the bad guys already?" Tim asked cheerfully.

"Not exactly." Luke dropped into a chair, his expression tired, worn, and hardly his usual self. "I need to talk to you."

"What's wrong? Are you not feeling well?" Tim frowned at his old friend, estimating how hard the flu might strike the elderly. Or the on the edge of being elderly as Luke was.

"I'm fine," Luke snapped. "I got a wire today. A missing person."

Tim hitched his hip on the side of his desk, a nervous shiver filling his stomach. "Go on."

"Here." Luke thrust a paper at him. "Read it."

He accepted the telegraph and glanced at it. In fear and dread, he read it all. "No," he muttered. "This is all wrong. Serena was going to Denver."

"She was *supposed* to go to California, Tim," Luke said on a groan. "And marry this Henry fellow. When she didn't get off the train, he sent wires to most every town along the train's route. He's looking for his bride. Serena. I – I wired back where she was."

"Luke!"

"I had to, doggone it." Luke covered his face with his hands. "As a lawman, I'm obliged to." He lifted his agonized yet hope-filled eyes to Tim. "Look, the gal likes you, you like her. Right? She's under no real obligation to go marry him.

Right? She's say no to him, yes to you, and all's well in Fort Riggins."

Tim stared at the floor. "Was she a Mail Order Bride?"

"It doesn't say."

"If she hasn't met him, then she may not be obligated to marry him. I don't know what the law might say about it."

Luke stood abruptly. "I'll ask Judge Miller. He's in town for a spell. Look, don't go off half-cocked, son. That Henry out there in California may have given up on her. And she doesn't remember him, anyway. We have time to work this out."

The prospect of Serena marrying someone else hovered over Tim like an evil shadow. He recalled the fierce determination of the Gardners that Serena continue her journey to Denver with them. *Why?* They had to know she was bound for California and marriage. So why divert her to Denver?

To protect her.

Dusk settled over the tall mountains as he paced slowly along the wooden sidewalk of Fort Riggins main street. He needed time to think about what he'd learned before going home to tell Serena that a man in California sought his missing bride.

And that *she* was that bride.

"Tim."

Stopping, Tim looked up to find Luke striding toward him. "Did you talk to the judge?"

Luke halted, smoothing his fingers down his mustache. "Sure did."

"You look pleased so he must have told you good news."

"He sure did." Luke turned to walk beside Tim. "If Serena hasn't signed her name on a marriage certificate, nor spoke her vows, she's not married, nor obligated to do so."

"That she verbally, or in a letter, agreed to marry this fellow doesn't apply?"

"Nope. Any gal can back out of a marriage agreement. Or any feller, for that matter."

"She's not obligated to marry him then." Tim felt a great weight lift from his shoulders. "You remember how that old couple insisted Serena go to Denver with them?"

"Yep."

"Maybe they talked her out of going to California," Tim mused. "They knew she was headed for trouble. Possibly?"

"That's my guess. They were awful insistent she head for Colorado with 'em."

"I have to tell Serena about this Henry looking for her. And why."

"That should be a real interesting conversation."

After supper, and while Luke helped Josephine in the kitchen, Tim held Serena's hand while leading her out onto the veranda. "There's something I need to tell you," he explained.

"I guessed as much," she replied. "I have something I need to confess to you."

"May I go first?" He sat in the chair beside her as the piano music from the saloon wafted across the nearly still, cool night air.

"Please." Serena's voice sounded strained, upset. She squeezed his hand in desperate fear. "I can't live with this secret any longer."

Alarm spread its evil fingers through his heart. "Tell me, Serena."

"I never lost my memories."

Whatever she'd planned to tell him, Tim hadn't expected that. "No?"

"No. Please understand, Tim, I hated the deceit. I felt I had no choice. I was terrified you'd send me to California."

"To Henry? The man you were supposed to marry?"

Serena went still. "How did you know that?" she whispered.

He chuckled. "Luke received a wire about a missing woman. Serena Stapleton. From a man in California named Henry searching for his missing bride."

"Oh." Tim heard her swallow. "Of course. I never thought he'd look for me."

"So you were to marry him?" Tim asked quietly. "And the Gardners persuaded you to not do so?"

"My father," Serena stood restlessly, pacing to the porch railing, "owed a businessman money. The man offered to cancel the debt if I married his son, Henry."

"Are you joking?" Outraged, Tim rose to stand beside her. "He *sold* you?"

"That's an excellent way of explaining it."

"So you never truly agreed to marry him."

"No. Mathilda and James persuaded me to accompany them to Denver. I'd live with them while they helped me find a husband – a man of *my* choosing. Not my father's."

"I can't blame you for wanting to escape."

She faced him. "Do you forgive me for deceiving you? And Josephine?"

Tim pulled her into his arms, holding her head against his shoulder. "I can't blame you for that, either. You had no idea what kind of people Ma and I were. You were scared. It's now quite clear why."

"I'm so sorry."

"Don't be." Lifting her chin, he kissed her tenderly, softly. "You did what you had to do."

Serena rested her cheek on his chest. "I thought you'd hate me for lying."

"If you'd lied about murdering someone in cold blood, we'd have a problem." He laughed softly. "Not for trying to protect yourself."

"I feared you'd put me on a train to Henry if you knew I was to marry him. That you'd feel obligated to."

"I thought you might be obligated to marry him," Tim replied, "but Luke talked to our local judge. You aren't."

Lifting her face, Serena laughed breathlessly. "Really? I don't have to?"

"Nope." Tim brushed a lock of her hair from her cheek. "You're free to marry whom you want."

Flinging her arms around his neck, Serena laughed again, kissing his cheek, his lips, anywhere she could reach. "That makes me so happy. And so *relieved*."

"Me, too." Tim kissed her soft lips slowly, lovingly, sweetly. "Because I'm falling in love with you."

"Good." Serena cupped his cheeks with both hands. "I'm falling in love with you, too."

"So what do you think will happen to your father now?"

She slid her arms from his neck but clasped his hands. "I-I don't … I can't truly care. I'm estranged from him, refused to call him my father. I suppose he'll have to pay his debt by working harder."

"And your mother?"

"Tim, I must write to her, tell her where I am, and what happened to me. She'll be so worried."

"Then write," Tim said cheerfully. "I'll pay the postage."

"You're so good to me."

"I believe you're good for me, Serena. Come on. Let's go tell my ma and Luke what's happening."

CHAPTER 9

"You've been cooped up in this house for too long," Josephine commented. "Walk to the bank with me."

"All right."

Since the evening two days ago when she confessed her deceit, Serena and Josephine had grown quite close. As did her rapidly growing love for Tim. With her burden lifted, Serena felt as light and free as a sparrow. As though she'd become an official member of the household, she helped not just around the house, but helped Josephine plant her garden behind the barn.

"Give me a moment to fetch my bonnet," Serena added, heading for her room.

The day had turned warm and sunny, a pleasant time to walk through the town. Serena and Josephine passed a few townsfolk who greeted them warmly, their eyes lit with curiosity upon seeing Serena. Even as Josephine offered introductions, Serena's attention was caught by the sight of two cowboys in tall hats and leather vests with guns on their hips riding past them. *Everything out here is so different from Boston.*

"That Mrs. Heller is a terrible gossip," Josephine said in a whisper as she and Serena continued on. "She'll be telling everyone in town about you."

"What's to tell?"

"Whatever she thinks will make the juiciest story."

"That's not very nice," Serena said, glancing over her shoulder. "Gossip for its own sake is wrong."

"That harpy lives for it."

The cowboys Serena noticed had reined in near the saloon but hadn't dismounted. She recalled dime novels that turned the American cowboys into heroes, thinking how much those two looked exactly like the sketches in the books. Then she followed Josephine into the bank, forgetting them.

She hung back as Josephine greeted the teller, glancing around the place. Beyond the teller's cage was a very large, strong-looking safe, a man in a suit working at a desk near it. A crystal vase with a few wilting flowers in it sat on a table near the front door. She glanced back at the sound of Josephine's laughter.

"This is Serena," Josephine said, half-turning to gesture at Serena. "She's staying with us."

"Very nice," the teller replied, smiling.

Behind Serena, the door opened. She paid scant attention as boots bonged hollowly on the wood flooring, only glancing aside as the cowboy stepped into her peripheral vision. At the same time, he glanced sidelong at her.

"You!" Serena screeched, recognizing him instantly.

Gregory Breyer's dark blue eyes widened as he, too, identified her as the woman who attacked him on the train. Though the lower half of his face was covered by a bandana, Serena saw his astonishment. And fear.

"A robbery!" the teller yelled. "We're being robbed."

Breyer yanked his gun from its holster, lifting it toward the teller. And Josephine. The six-gun's coughing bark ripped through the small room. Josephine cried out, stumbled back, then slid to the floor. Red bloomed on her sleeve and bodice.

"No!" Serena screamed.

Wheeling, she seized the vase, lifting it, consumed by her rage, her grief that yet another friend had been hurt by this terrible man. Breyer spun toward her, his gun up, aiming, preparing to fire, to kill her as he killed Josephine.

Serena moved faster.

Swinging the vase, water spraying across her bonnet, Serena cracked it against the side of Breyer's head. He stumbled, staggered toward her, the gun falling to the wooden floor with a thudding sound. Her fury unabated, the heavy vase still intact, she swung it in a backhanded blow, striking him again. This time, Breyer fell across his gun, and lay still.

The teller and the bank manager rushed to Josephine. "Get the doctor and the sheriff," the manager gasped. "Run."

The teller obeyed, passed Serena by to dash into the street. Breathing hard, Serena stared at the silent form of her victim. As wild yells, shouts, and gunfire erupted from outside, she dropped the vase to hurry to Josephine's side.

"How bad?"

The manager helped Josephine, pale but groaning and very much alive, to sit up and lean against the wall. "It's her arm," he replied, "I need something to stop her bleeding."

Serena tore a long strips of cloth from her gown, and helped the man to wrap them around Josephine's arm. Josephine smiled wryly, glancing at the unconscious outlaw. "You are a little spitfire," she murmured.

"Hush now," Serena ordered. "Tim will be here soon."

Within minutes, Tim did indeed arrive with the teller behind him. "Ma, oh no, sir, let me get in there."

While Tim examined Josephine, Serena crouched worriedly beside him yet watched as the two bank employees tied Breyer's hands behind his back. "Get his gun," the manager ordered. "Good, let's tie his legs, too. All nice and tidy for the sheriff."

"I have to get you to the office, Ma," Tim said, his voice less urgent.

"Help me up," Josephine ordered.

"I'll carry you."

"Tim, don't –"

Ignoring her protests, Tim scooped Josephine into his arms. Stepping around the outlaw, Serena held the door open for him. Outside, men stood in a loose group, talking excitedly, gesturing at someone lying on the ground. Serena caught sight of Luke in their midst, and he appeared to be handcuffing a cowboy's hands behind his back.

"Luke," Tim called, passing the group by. "The other one is in the bank, tied up."

"Almost no need for me as a lawman," Luke griped cheerfully, standing. He turned sober at the sight of Josephine. "Is she all right?"

"She will be."

With only a single lamp burning beside her, Serena sat beside Josephine's bed as the woman slept. The outlaw's bullet had passed cleanly through Josephine's upper arm without breaking her bone. Tim sutured her wounds closed, and she now slept under the effects of laudanum. Tim and Luke talked downstairs in the kitchen, but Serena didn't want to leave Josephine's side.

"Come eat something." Tim spoke softly from the doorway. "She'll sleep through the night."

"She almost died."

"Almost. But she didn't. Her arm may be stiff the rest of her life, but she'll recover fully."

Rising, Serena lowered the lamp's wick, then paced quietly across the room to him. "Are you sure?"

He kissed her briefly. "I'm the doc."

Accompanying him downstairs, their hands linked, Serena scented bacon frying. In the kitchen, Luke hovered over the stove, the table set for three. Sliced bread lay on the plates. He eyed them as they entered and offered Serena a crooked grin.

"Bacon is about all I can cook. So we're having bacon sandwiches for dinner."

"I'm not very hungry." Serena wearily sat at the table, resting her chin on her hands.

"You need to eat," Tim scolded her lightly. "You haven't eaten all day."

"I'd add you need to keep up your strength," Luke commented with a wink. "But today you showed you have plenty of that."

"What do you mean?"

"You took out a wanted man all by your lonesome." Luke winked. "There's a hefty reward coming your way. The marshals are planning to wire it to your account."

"I don't have one," Serena said, looking at Tim in confusion. "How much is this reward?"

"According to the marshals, the Breyer Brothers are high on their wanted list," Luke answered, turning the bacon with a fork. "One thousand dollars for Gregory Breyer alone."

Serena laughed in disbelief. "That's not possible." She caught Tim's eyes, took in his confident smile. "You're joking. Right?"

"He's not." Tim took her hand. "What you did today not just saved many lives, but you single-handedly captured a wanted outlaw. The Breyer Brothers won't be robbing trains and banks any longer."

"But." Serena glanced helplessly from Tim to Luke and back again. "I didn't catch the other one."

"No, that was accomplished by townsfolk," Luke replied. "Smart fellers realized what was going on when the shot went off in the bank, grabbed him off his horse. They'll split Harold's reward money."

Still disbelieving, Serena shook her head. "The bank's people captured him."

Luke snorted, glaring over his shoulder. "*You* knocked him out cold. *They* only tied him up. If you hadn't, Breyer would have shot every one of you, *including* you. Now quit fussing and enjoy being a wealthy woman."

An idea passed quickly into Serena's mind as Luke doled out bacon onto bread. "I should use it to help pay my father's debt."

"Oh, no, you don't," Tim snapped. "That money is yours, girl. You'll use it for what you want and need. He can pay his own debts."

"Buy a house," Luke stated, sitting down. "Live here until you find a decent husband."

Serena looked at Tim, and he looked at her, then smiled. "Maybe I've found one."

Tim leaned over to kiss her, grinning. "Now you'll think I'm only after your money."

"What will I do with one thousand dollars?" Serena mused.

"Whatever you want, dear," Josephine answered, busy cooking at the stove, her left arm in a sling. "Perhaps invest in real estate. This town will grow, you mark my words. People will settle the area, buy land. It's a perfect cattle ranching region."

"True."

As time passed and Josephine healed, Serena had fallen fully and truly in love with Tim. And he with her. As spring passed into summer, they spent every evening on the veranda, talking of the future, of children, of the possibilities.

"Has he asked you to marry him yet?" Josephine asked, sitting down with Serena.

"Not yet." She smiled. "I think he's waiting for the perfect moment."

Josephine patted her hand, smiling. "I'm so glad you came here, Serena. *How* you came to our home wasn't exactly conventional, but I'm very glad you entered our lives."

"I am, too." Serena gripped Josephine's fingers. "I wrote to the Gardners, told them everything. Maybe they can come for a visit."

"And your mother." Josephine chuckled. "I'd love to meet her. Not your father, however. I'm not sure I can welcome him under my roof."

"I should forgive him, I suppose." Serena drew a deep breath. "One day."

Tim's voice called from the front sitting room. "Hello? The train arrived a short while ago."

"We're in the kitchen," Josephine called back.

Tim stepped into the doorway, his eyes only for Serena. Bending, he kissed her. "While I was at the train, the station master handed me a wire. It's for you."

"For me?" Serena took it and unfolded the paper. "It's from my mother." She grinned in excitement, reading the brief lines. "She's coming here. I can't believe it."

"That's wonderful," Josephine exclaimed. "And your father?"

"She didn't say. Only that she'll arrive in a few weeks."

"So I get to meet my future ma-in-law." Tim kissed her again, grinning.

"You haven't asked me to marry you yet." Serena sniffed. "I'm a wealthy woman. You might just be after my money, you know. Maybe I don't want to marry you after all."

Tim feigned hurt. "And you said you loved me."

"Not if you only want me for my money."

"I have to marry you first, then get your money. Marry me, sweetheart?"

Serena, laughing, pushed him away. "Stop being silly. And if you don't ask me to marry you in a romantic fashion, I certainly will refuse."

"Then I'd best get to planning a romantic setting, shouldn't I?"

A sharp knock sounded at the front door, a hard rapping as though the visitor was angry, impatient, or both. Tim's brows rose as he glanced between Serena and Josephine. "Are we expecting guests?"

"No," Josephine replied. "Luke would walk right in."

Tim left the kitchen, muttering something akin to breaking that man's bad habits. Absently, Serena wondered if their visitor had come to call Tim for a medical emergency. However, the stranger's loud voice demanded, carrying clearly to the kitchen. "Miss Stapleton. Is she here?"

Alarmed, Serena exchanged a confused glance with Josephine, and stood up.

"And who might you be?" Tim asked as Serena, followed by Josephine, stepped from the kitchen.

"I'm Henry Dunstable," the obnoxious man snapped. "I'm told she's here."

Serena gasped. Dunstable's dark eyes passed Tim to fix on her. He grinned with menacing pleasure. "Ah, you're quite the beauty as your father said. Come on, let's go."

"Excuse me?" Tim growled, stepping between Dunstable and Serena. "She's not going anywhere. Especially with you."

"She's my fiancée." Dunstable swept by him as if he owned the house, crossing the sitting room toward Serena. "I've come to claim her, take her home. Come on, I said."

Serena snatched her arm away when he tried to seize it. "I'm not marrying you, sir. Nor am I going with you."

Dunstable's lips peeled back, and he sent a half glance over his shoulder as Tim stepped up behind him. "Your father gave his word, woman. Who are you to gainsay him?"

Tim shifted his head and mouthed the name "Luke" at Josephine. She nodded jerkily, then ducked past Dunstable to rush from the house. Serena, scared yet defiant, glared at the short, balding man with the obnoxious attitude. When he reached for her again, she slapped his hand away.

"Don't you touch me," she grated. "My father may have agreed to this travesty, but I have not consented. You have no right to come here and drag me from this house. Now, leave."

Dunstable stared as though she'd just spoken a vile string of oaths. "I have every right to take you as my bride," he snapped. "Your father signed away your consent. Now come with me."

Tim seized Dunstable's shoulder and spun him around. "Get out of my house," he bellowed.

For answer, Dunstable punched Tim hard in the mouth. Stumbling back, stunned, Tim fought to not fall. Serena, silent, lunged at Dunstable, using her fingernails like daggers. She clawed at his eyes and his face. Dunstable roared in pain and fury, knocking her to the floor with a powerful sweep of his arm.

Tim launched himself at Dunstable, punching the man's head, face, with wild yet short swings of his fists. Dunstable fell back, defending himself, yet clearly outmatched by Tim's rage, youth, and strength. Sitting up, scrambling to her feet, Serena watched for an opening in which she, too, could join the fray.

In a swift, unforeseen move, Dunstable kicked Tim's legs out from under him. Tim fell on his hip and side, yet fought to rise and fight again, his face twisted in fierce determination. Dunstable stepped back, his hand reaching under his coat. Serena instantly recognized the triumph in his dark eyes.

"Tim!"

Serena lunged. She struck Dunstable with all her slender weight, knocking him off balance even as she fought to seize the gun from his hand. Without truly remembering her fight with Gregory Breyer, she punched Dunstable, hard, in his throat. Gagging, choking, Dunstable fought to stay on his feet, trying to aim the gun.

Both Serena and Dunstable went down under Tim's full weight.

"Get the gun!" Serena screeched, hitting Dunstable in his face again. Her hand and wrist felt as though she'd broken both, but she struggled to get on top of Dunstable to hold him down.

Her skirt tore with a sharp rip as she slammed her knee into Dunstable's gut. Tim, his right hand gripping Dunstable's wrist to keep the gun pointed up, was unable to use his left fist effectively due to Serena. Still, he hit Dunstable under his chin, and snapped the man's head.

Dunstable collapsed.

Tim seized the gun from his lax hand, and, breathing heavily, stepped off Dunstable.

"Here." He pulled Serena up and tucked her under his arm. For several long moments, Serena and Tim simply looked at Dunstable as he lay, breathing raggedly, on the rug.

"My little spitfire." Tim shook his head and grinned. "I'm sure glad you're on my side."

Serena sniffed. "I get angry when someone hurts someone I love."

Luke, a rifle in his hands, charged through the doorway. He skidded to a halt on the bearskin rug, gaping. "Did you –"

"Yeah." Tim took Serena with him as he headed for the sofa. "Serena did her share."

"You all are gonna make me lose my job," Luke complained, rolling Dunstable over to wrench his arms behind him, and handcuff him. "You citizens taking the law in your hands, what does that leave me to do?"

"Sit in your office and read the paper." Tim held Serena close. "Court my mother."

At that moment, Josephine, her face waxy pale, hurried inside. And stopped. She stared at Dunstable, Tim, Luke and finally at Serena.

"You certainly made a mess out of my nice house," she snapped, her right hand on her hip. "Just look at this." She gestured at the overturned table, the broken oil lamp and the oil staining the rug.

"I'll clean it up," Serena said, nestling into Tim's shoulder. "I helped make the mess."

"You sure made a mess out of that man's face." Josephine commented, standing over Luke and Dunstable.

"He was about to shoot us. And he made me mad."

Josephine shook her head. "Remind me to never make you angry, dear."

"What did you say?" Luke demanded, striding to the sofa.

"What did I say?" Tim asked, looking up.

"What's this about courting your mother?"

"I don't want to be courted," Josephine cried.

"I said I *don't* want you courting my mother," Tim replied with a smirk.

"No, no, son, that's not what you said." Luke snapped, glowering. "You said I get to sit and read the paper and *court your mother. I heard* you."

"You're getting senile, old man. Starting to hear things."

"Oh, stop teasing him," Serena murmured, comfortable against Tim's shoulder. "You never courted me."

"No, I sure didn't." Tim kissed her brow. "I should rectify that. Take you out to dinner, woo you, ask you to marry me."

"At one dinner?" Serena lifted her face to stare. "That's not courting."

'Well, it's jumping from one dinner into a marriage proposal. Easy. Right?"

Serena sat up. "I'm going back to Boston. I have wealth, you know. I'll have men falling all over me."

Tim seized her hand. "Ah, but you love *me*, sweetheart. Marry me, and I'll make you the happiest of women."

"That's hardly romantic," Serena protested. "I want to be romanced."

"Well," Tim drawled, "you can accept my proposal, or marry that gentleman yonder on the floor. In handcuffs."

Serena groaned. "Such a choice. All right."

"All right what?"

"I'll marry that gentleman yonder. In handcuffs."

Laughing, Tim swept her into his arms, kissing her, taking her breath away. "Marry me, my lady love. Marry me and make me the happiest of men."

Serena, her arms around his neck, nuzzled her face under his jaw. "I love you, Tim. Yes, I'll marry you."

"Great," Luke drawled. "Now that's out of the way, so it's my turn. Jo, honey, will you marry me?"

The End

CONTINUE READING ...

Thank you for reading *Escaping the Marriage Contract!* Are you wondering **what to read next?** Why not read *The Bride's Arrangement?* **Here's a peek for you:**

Ryan Bastion held his six-month-old son close as he paced the floor of the ranch house. Baby Jed was miserable, crying and twisting in Ryan's arms. Ryan patted and crooned and jiggled the little boy, but nothing seemed to comfort him.

Ryan was miserable, too. As the owner of a ranch, he worked hard. As a single father, he had to work even harder. Frustration swelled within him. He almost felt like throwing back his head and joining Jed in crying and howling. He was exhausted.

It had been a long six months since his wife died in childbirth. Not only was the grief overwhelming, but he was also hit with total responsibility for taking care of infant Jed's needs. His neighbor Maudie Olsen and her family had helped as much as possible, and he thanked God for them, but they couldn't be here all day and night.

Fortunately, Jed was mostly a good baby, and nights spent like this had been rare. Unfortunately, Jed was teething now and had been fussy for the last week. Ryan was nearly at the end of his rope trying to comfort the baby.

Maybe he should consider Jess's idea. His best friend, Jess Chapman, had been talking about Mail Order Brides the other day. Ryan had laughed at him at first, but the more he thought about it, the more it made sense. He would have someone here at all times to take care of Jed, someone who could cook his meals and clean his house. And the house wouldn't be so darn empty, like a tomb.

That was a crazy idea, of course. To marry a complete stranger was ludicrous. If he wanted to remarry, he could marry a local girl.

That idea somehow felt repugnant to him, though. He had no intention of this being anything more than a marriage in name only if he gave in to this crazy concept. He could explain that clearly in any letters he would exchange with his prospective bride. He'd known the few local girls for much of his life, and he wouldn't be comfortable talking about that with them. They would expect romance, and he wasn't willing to provide that. He still loved Molly and he always would. Intimacy with another woman seemed intolerable. No, this marriage was to be treated like a business deal.

As Jed wound up and squalled even louder, Ryan made up his mind. It was a risk, but one he thought he should take. Yep, he nodded. He was going to get himself a Mail Order Bride.

Visit HERE To Read More!

https://ticahousepublishing.com/mail-order-brides.html

THANKS FOR READING!

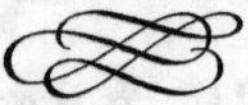

If you **love Mail Order Bride Romance, Visit Here**

https://wesrom.subscribemenow.com/

to find out about all **New Susannah Calloway Romance Releases! We will let you know as soon as they become available!**

If you enjoyed *Escaping the Marriage Contract,* would you kindly take a couple minutes to leave a positive review on Amazon? It only takes a moment, and positive reviews truly make a difference. Thank you so much! I appreciate it!

Turn the page to discover more Mail Order Bride Romances just for you!

ABOUT THE AUTHOR

Susannah has always been intrigued with the Western movement - prairie days, mail-order brides, the gold rush, frontier life! As a writer, she's excited to combine her love of story with her love of all that is Western. Presently, Susannah lives in Wyoming with her hubby and their three amazing children.

www.ticahousepublishing.com
contact@ticahousepublishing.com